T0197507

THE CREATOR

AND

ITS

CREATIONS

Z

Archway Publishing books may be ordered through booksellers or by contacting:

Archway Publishing
1663 Liberty Drive
Bloomington, IN 47403
www.archwaypublishing.com
844-669-3957

Because of the dynamic nature of the Internet, any web addresses or links contained in this book may have changed since publication and may no longer be valid. The views expressed in this work are solely those of the author and do not necessarily reflect the views of the publisher, and the publisher hereby disclaims any responsibility for them.

Any people depicted in stock imagery provided by Getty Images are models, and such images are being used for illustrative purposes only.
Certain stock imagery © Getty Images.

ISBN: 978-1-6657-3908-5 (sc)
ISBN: 978-1-6657-3909-2 (hc)
ISBN: 978-1-6657-3907-8 (e)

Interior Image Credit: Nora Charmaine Quattrochi

Print information available on the last page.

Archway Publishing rev. date: 05/03/2023

Thank you for sharing your blessings.
A percentage of "The Creator and Its Creations"
yearly proceeds will go towards the gift
of clean water throughout our Earth.
Your purchase created infinite connections
And the span of gratitude is unbounded.

Thank YOU!

For my Mothers

For my Fathers

For my Sisters

For my Brothers

And For All The Webs We Weave

Once upon a place and once upon a time,

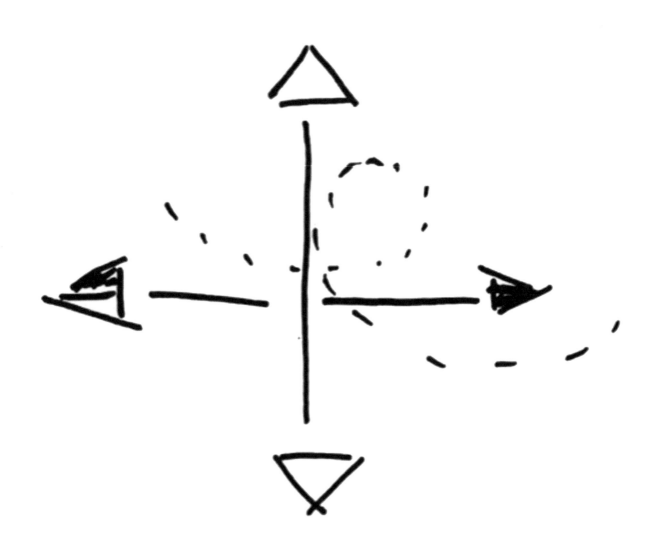

there lived a Creator

and all its creations.

There were gold ones

And cosmic ones

even ones with many moons.

But of all the Creator's creations,

Its favorite was green, white, and blue.

Yes, of all the Creator's creations, the one that it liked best,

Was the one it had spent much time on,

It was the one that it called X.

Yes, with X the Creator was happy; there was something truly special . . .

about the way that X had changed each day,

making every moment magical.

Yes, the Creator created creations; it was what it was meant to do.

Some would pass quickly through their phases,

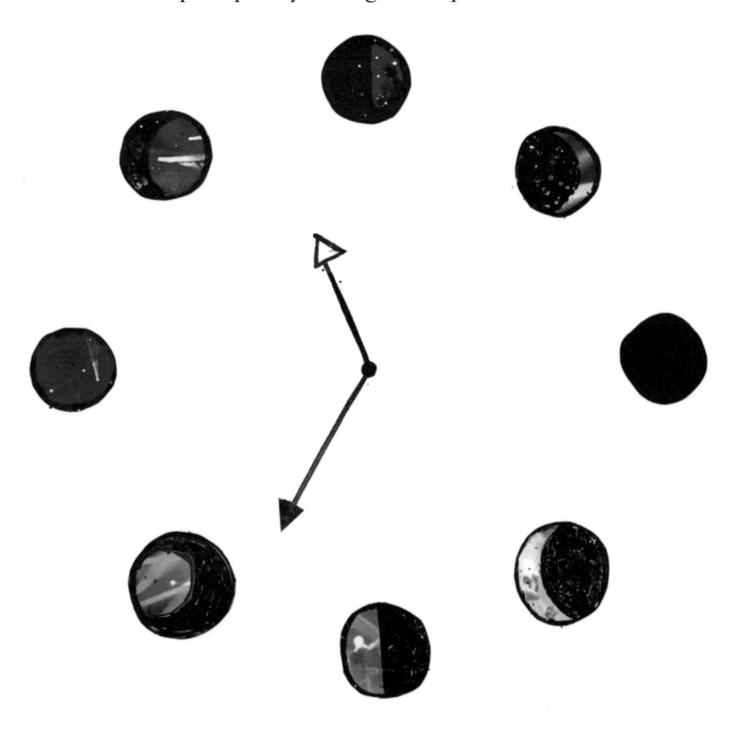

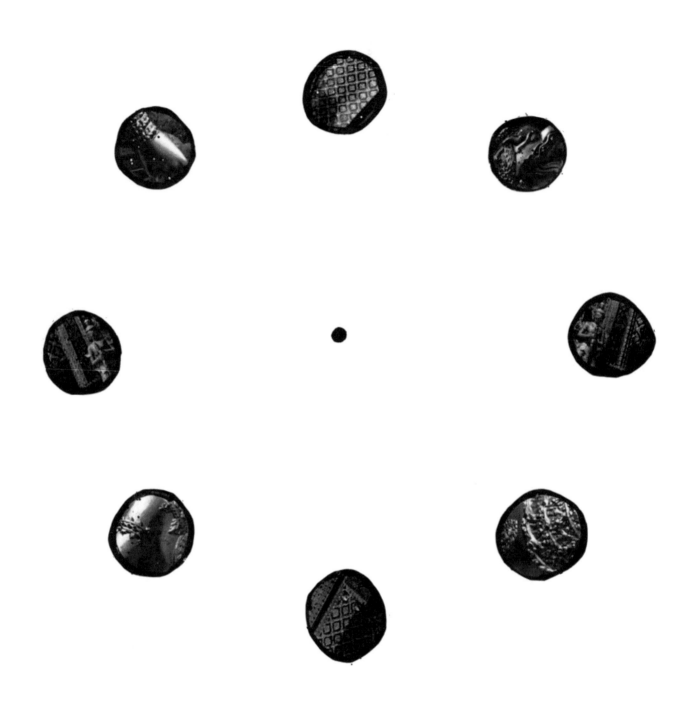

while others stayed brand-new.

So when the morning came when X didn't seem so light.

That the Creator noticed something
different, a darkening in X's eyes.

It hated to admit it; no, it didn't want it to be true.

That the Creator would have to let X go—

there was nothing left to do.

The Creator had to remove its creation;
release it from time and space.

But it did so with sadness, tears
rolling down its face.

The Creator had said goodbye before, but
this time it didn't seem quite right.

To walk away from its dearest friend as
their last day turned to night.

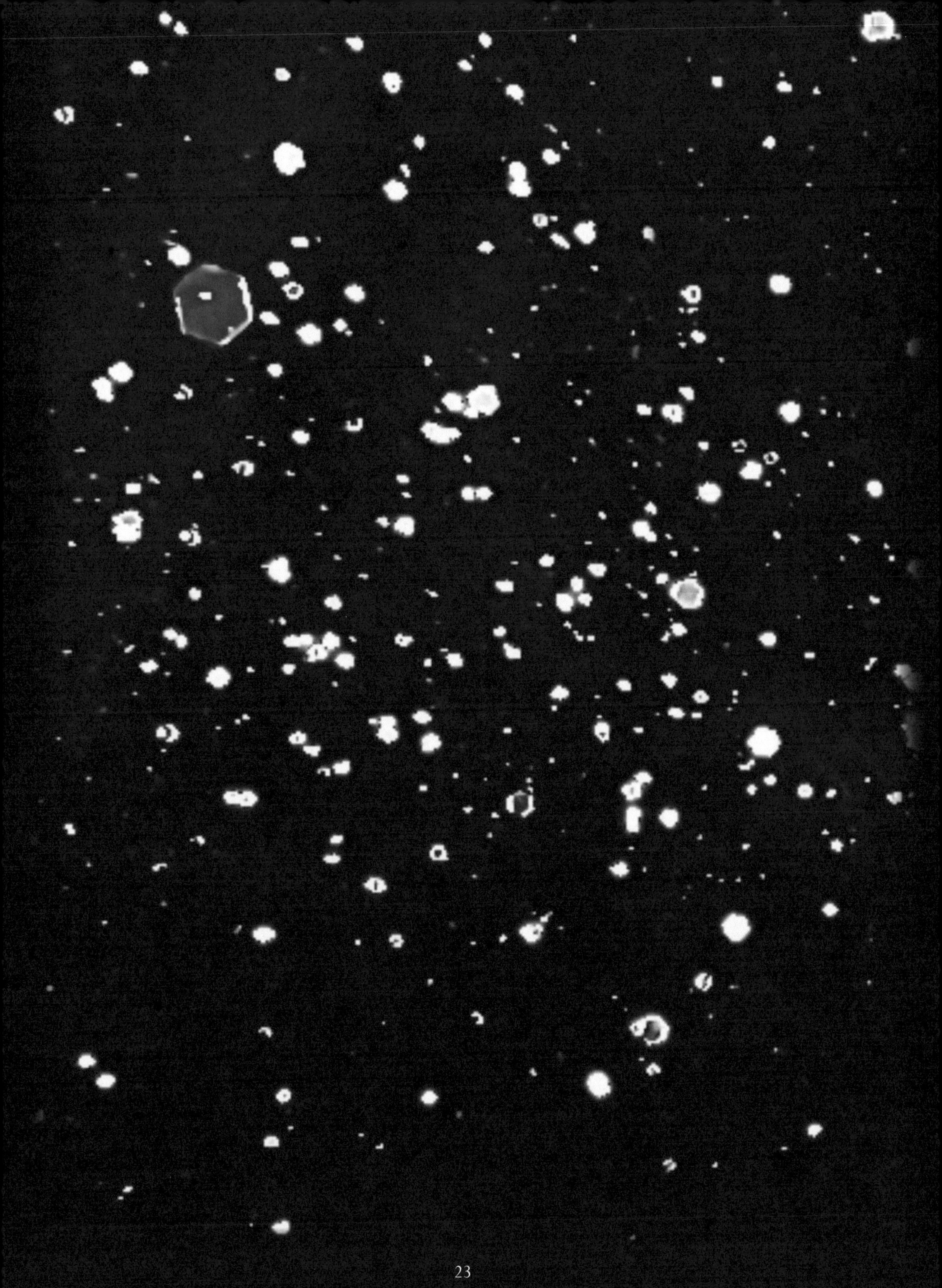

But the Creator kept creating, yes, creations came and went, but as much as it tried to deny it,

It couldn't help but to think of X.

It tried as hard as it could, it didn't want to give up, to recreate its favorite creation, but it didn't have much luck.

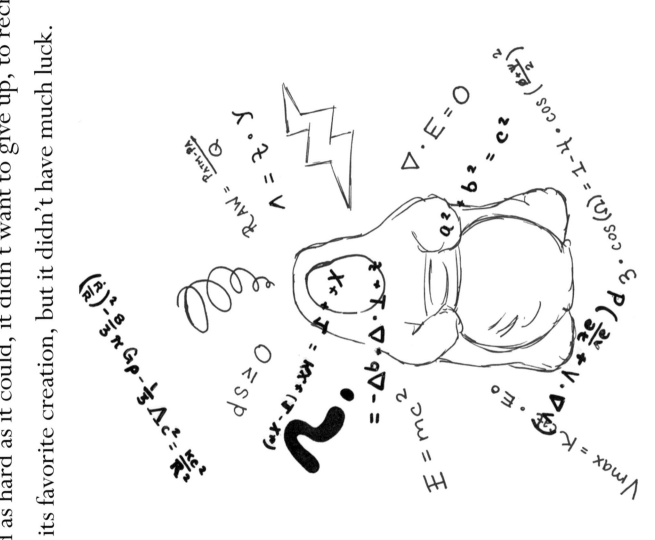

No, no creation had come back, no not one time. It had never seen a creation again once its power had fully died.

So, one day when the Creator was sitting, underneath the shade of a tree

It couldn't believe what it was seeing, a miracle in its view, X was approaching.

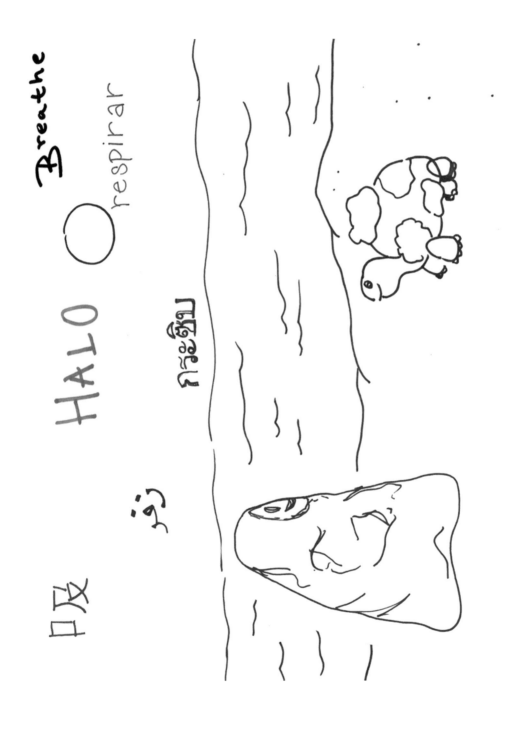

Breathe

Halo ◯ respirar

呼吸

Each step X took slowly, inhaling a deeper breath each time…

29

"Hello friend, I've missed you." The Creator said

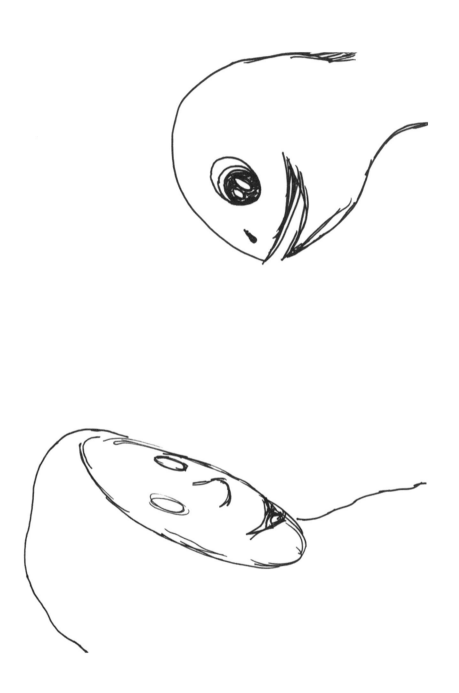

As X spoke the words: "I told you I'd be fine."